Littlenose to the Rescue

"I don't think I could have enough honey *ever*, Two-Eyes," said Littlenose to his pet mammoth. Ice Age boys never had sweets, cakes, or anything made from sugar. Honey was a great treat, a reward when Littlenose had been extra good, which wasn't very often. So Littlenose attempted to capture a bees' nest, but swiftly retreated from that escapade. Then he tried feeding the bees and guarding their nest, but that didn't work either. He never got his honey – but his understanding of the bees delivered Father and himself from a fate much worse than being stung.

Of course, no one believed Littlenose had saved them. Then, as now, small boys were not always appreciated, especially by their parents.

John Grant created his endearing character for Jackanory, and Littlenose has an appreciative audience of viewers and readers. *Littlenose to the Rescue* is the sixth instalment of the adventures of this Ice Age hero.

Littlenose
to the Rescue

John Grant

Illustrated by the author

as told in Jackanory

British Broadcasting Corporation

Published by the British Broadcasting Corporation
35 Marylebone High Street, London W1M 4AA
ISBN 0 563 12879 8
First published 1975
© John Grant 1975
Printed in England by John Blackburn Ltd, Leeds

Littlenose the Bee Keeper

During the Ice Age, boys like Littlenose ate many of the same foods as we do today. They had meat and fish as well as fruit and vegetables, but they also ate things we would never dream of. Caterpillars for instance. But there was something that Littlenose knew nothing about, and which we probably couldn't do without. And that was sugar. Littlenose never had sweets to eat, or jam, or sticky buns, or anything made from sugar. Instead he ate honey. Honey was found by taking it from the nests of wild bees. Collecting honey was almost as dangerous as hunting rhinoceros or elk. The bees may have been small, but they were as ferocious in their own small way as sabre-toothed tigers. So, honey was eaten only as a treat or as a reward for something special that Littlenose might have done, like staying out of trouble for a whole day, or washing his hands without being told more than once.

One afternoon Littlenose was sitting with Two-Eyes his pet mammoth under his favourite tree nibbling at a morsel of honeycomb. He made it last as long as he could, then popped the last crumb into his mouth, licked his fingers and sighed.

"I don't think I could get enough honey *ever*, Two-Eyes," he said. "If only it grew on trees like fruit, or if bees hadn't stings. The black bears have no problems getting honey. Their fur is so thick and shaggy that the bees' stings can't even touch them. They have long sharp claws for cutting open the honeycomb, and are tall enough to reach up to the highest bees' nest." He turned to Two-Eyes. "Nothing personal," he said, "but it would have been more use if you had been a bear instead of a mammoth."

He was still thinking about honey as he ate his midday meal, and Father had to lean across and shake him to get his attention. "Mother's talking to you. Wake up and listen," he snapped.

"Your own special corner of the cave is a disgrace," said Mother. "It's like a bears' den. You can spend the afternoon tidying it." Again Littlenose sighed. There were times when he felt that life was just one

bother after another! But, as the afternoon passed, he began rather to enjoy himself. He found all sorts of treasures that he had given up for lost. Some coloured pebbles. A small carved bone. A drawing of a beaver on a piece of birch bark, and several spare flints. But the thing which delighted him most was his hunting robe. Now he put it on and strutted up and down admiring himself. As he did so a wonderful idea began to form in his mind. Honey! Black bears! Shaggy fur! Furry hunting robe! Bundling everything back into his corner, he rushed outside shouting to Two-Eyes: "I've got it. We can get all the honey we want!"

The plan was so simple that he wondered how he hadn't thought of it before! If he wrapped himself up tightly in his fur robe and pulled the hood well over his face he would be as well protected from the bees as a bear in its shaggy skin. His spear was as sharp as a bear's claws for cutting up honeycomb, and he knew where there was a bees' nest not far from the cave. No time like the present for putting his plan into action!

With Two-Eyes following at a discreet distance, Littlenose set off into the woods. They soon came in sight of the tree where the bees nested, and Littlenose could see bees buzzing in and out. He put on his hunting robe, wrapping it tightly about him. Next he pulled the hood completely over his head and face. Then, taking a firm grip of his spear through the robe, he cautiously approached the tree. Right away he realised that he had forgotten something important. The shaggy fur of a bear has two holes . . . directly opposite its eyes. Littlenose just couldn't see where he was going! But he blundered and stumbled towards the tree, guided by the buzzing of the bees. The noise grew louder as he approached and as the bees began to wonder what this weird creature was, obviously up to no good. It was hot and stuffy with the robe right over his face, so Littlenose paused for a moment, and discovered another important thing about a bear's fur. It hasn't got an opening for its legs to poke through. And one of the bees, bolder than the rest, discovered the gap in Littlenose's covering. It flew underneath the robe, and at that moment Littlenose decided to lean against a tree for a moment to get his bearings. He leant against the bee, which did what you'd expect. It stung him. With a yell, Littlenose threw off the hood and ran.

Later, Littlenose again sat down with Two-Eyes to think about honey and the best way of getting it. A long time ago Uncle Redhead had shown him a place where bees nested among high rocks by a river. Uncle Redhead had lit a very smoky fire at the foot of the rocks, and the smoke so confused the bees that he was able to climb up and take dripping hunks of comb before they knew what was happening. But, Littlenose knew that whatever silly things he might do, lighting fires at the foot of trees must never be one of them. It could lead to a forest fire. None of the high rocks he knew had so far appealed to bees as a

nesting place. Reluctantly he decided to forget the whole idea, and ran off to play.

A few days later Littlenose went with Father to catch some fish for the evening meal. They were returning along the river bank when Father suddenly said, "We're in luck. Look! That's a swarm of bees. And a swarm of bees overhead means good luck is coming your way. Quiet now. Here they come."

With a loud droning the swarm swept round over their heads and disappeared beyond the river bank. Littlenose straightened up with relief. "Where are they going?" he asked.

"To find a new home," said Father. "When the nest becomes too crowded, some of the bees set off under the leadership of their own queen to make a new nest. It's very lucky for a swarm to fly over a person's head."

"Why?" said Littlenose.

"Because it is. That's why!" said Father impatiently. "Now, don't dawdle or we'll be late getting home."

After supper Littlenose wandered out of the cave to play before bed-time. He thought about the bee swarm as he walked towards the river and along the bank, not going anywhere in particular. It was growing dusk and he was about to go home when he realised that he was close to the spot where he and Father had seen the bees. He climbed up and over the bank and pushed his way carefully through the undergrowth. He could see very little, and decided to wait until daylight. But, as he turned to go he heard humming. Not loud, and sounding rather sleepy. It was coming from a jumbled heap of boulders. This must be the place the bees had chosen for a new nest. Littlenose decided to return in the morning to investigate further. For already wonderful ideas were racing through his head and he wanted to waste no time in putting them into practice.

Before breakfast next day Littlenose was up, out of the cave and running along the river bank. He wondered if the bees were really there. Maybe his ears had played tricks on him. Maybe all he had heard was the wind in the tall grass. He crept through the dew, studying the boulders carefully. He couldn't hear a thing, but when he moved closer he saw some movement. From a wide, deep cleft between two rocks a bee crawled out into the sunlight. It was followed by two others. Then more and more emerged, pausing for a moment before flying off to begin their day's work. They looked as if they had settled down to stay.

After breakfast, Littlenose sat with Two-Eyes under his favourite tree and explained his scheme. "These are going to be *my* special bees," he said. "I will protect them from bears, and I will bring them flowers so that they will not get tired out flying around looking for them. They'll get to know me, and won't grudge me the odd drop of honey."

Which shows that Littlenose, even by

Neanderthal standards, was a somewhat simple soul. But he was as good as his word, standing on guard with spear and gathering great armfuls of flowers which he laid out at a safe distance from the rock pile. After about a week he thought that the bees should be settled in, so he paid them a visit. It was a bitter disappointment. He could find no sign of honey, and worse still the bees were very discourteous. They did not seem to know him and he arrived home nursing several painful stings. The same thing happened a week later, and the week after that, so that he came to the sad conclusion that bees were ungrateful creatures. "After all that I've done for them," he said to Two-Eyes. "They can find their own flowers from now on!" And so Littlenose very soon forgot all about the bees.

For one thing it was not all play being a Neanderthal boy. Littlenose had to do his bit in hunting for food with Father as well as helping Mother about the cave. Mother actually preferred him helping Father.

One afternoon the Old Man, leader of the tribe, called a meeting of all hunters and learner-hunters, which included Littlenose.

"I've just had word," he said, "that the Straightnoses have been seen in the district. We must be particularly careful not to attract their attention. If they do not know that we are here they will go on their way. But if we are discovered. . . ."

His audience looked at one another and shuddered. The Old Man didn't need to say any more. Everyone knew that the Straightnoses were more dangerous than the woolly rhinoceros and more cunning than the sabre-toothed tiger! The Straightnoses didn't live respectably in caves, but roamed the plains and hills following the game herds. This made them doubly dangerous, as you could never be absolutely sure where they would turn up next.

The Old Man spoke again. "We must go out to hunt or we shall starve. But to avoid attracting attention, hunting parties must be no larger than two. And, of course, there will be no fires lit and only hunters may leave the vicinity of the caves for the duration of the emergency." Now the tribe put out their fires and barricaded their cave entrances. Littlenose didn't feel much like sitting around a cold cave for days on end,

and was overjoyed when Father said, "You and I are going out as a hunting party, leaving at dawn tomorrow. And for goodness sake don't do anything silly or we're liable to be the ones being hunted . . . by the Straightnoses."

The hunting proved very successful, at least to begin with, and they soon had a fine bag of rabbits, hare and other small game. They were making for home, laden down, and cautiously scanning the land in front of them for Straightnose tracks when Littlenose glanced back the way they had come. Next moment he shouted: "Quick! Look!" Father took one look and started to run, beckoning Littlenose to follow. He too had seen two distant man-shaped specks moving rapidly in their direction with the unmistakable loping stride of a Straightnose hunter tracking game. The game was Littlenose and Father! But they had a head start, and glancing back Littlenose saw that they were drawing away.

Then, disaster! Father put his foot on a loose stone, and next moment he was sitting on the ground clutching his ankle. He tried to stand, and with a loud yell sat down again. "It's sprained," he groaned. "Run,

Littlenose. Save yourself."

"I'll try to draw them away from you," said Littlenose, "they're gaining fast." He jumped up and circled away from where Father lay in the long grass, trying desperately to think of a plan. Then he saw something familiar about a nearby heap of boulders. The Straightnoses were very close as Littlenose, hidden in the long grass, picked up a heavy stone and threw it, not at the Straightnoses, but into a clump of bushes where it landed with a loud rustle. Instantly the Straightnoses turned towards the sound. Littlenose threw another stone, and another, each time in another place and each time the Straightnoses made for the spot, thinking that Father and Littlenose lay hidden there. What they didn't realise was that Littlenose was leading them closer and closer to the rock pile. They were close beside it when Littlenose threw his last stone. He had never thrown a stone so carefully in all his life. The stone whizzed through the air . . . and straight into the wide cleft he had recognized. The place where the bees had made their nest. They had been unfriendly when Littlenose brought them flowers. They were wild with rage when he threw a large stone right into their home. With a ferocious buzzing they rushed out. They didn't see Littlenose hidden in the undergrowth, but they did see the two Straightnose hunters. Next moment, screaming and yelling in the middle of a cloud of angry insects, the Straightnoses were running for their lives, leaping up and down and waving their arms as they did.

As the noise died away, Father leaned on Littlenose's shoulder and hobbled the last short bit of the journey home. He didn't really understand why the Straightnoses had fled, and Littlenose didn't think he would be believed if he told him.

Littlenose the Magician

In the days when Littlenose lived the most important person in the tribe was the Old Man. But, only a little less important was the Doctor. He looked after the sick, as you might expect, but he had other important duties as well.

For instance, he foretold the future. This he did by watching pictures in the fire, or by observing the flight of birds. But his favourite method was to take out a pack of white birch bark squares with strange markings on them. He spread them out on a flat rock, then turned them up one at a time, muttering as he did so. The people would crowd round his cave saying: "He is going to make a prediction." Then a meeting would be called later in the day at which the Doctor would raise his arms and pronounce in a solemn voice something like: "There is going to be a hard winter!" And considering this was the Ice Age he had never been wrong!

Littlenose didn't think much of either the Doctor's nasty-tasting medicines or his fortune telling, but he was filled with awe at the Doctor's other job, that of Tribal Magician. He had only the vaguest idea what magic was, and he had never seen the Doctor actually perform any, but he heard a lot about it. He knew, for instance, that he could make a coloured pebble vanish and produce it from someone's ear; he had heard that with the right magic words a handful of old bones could become a bouquet of flowers; and there was the story of a rabbit which the Doctor had produced from an empty fur hood. Someone had once asked why he didn't use his magic to help in useful things like hunting and rain-making as the Straightnoses did. The Doctor was horrified. "It is not for us to meddle with the powers of darkness," he said warningly. "Look what it's done for the Straightnoses. You wouldn't want to end up like them, would you?" And as that was the last thing anyone wanted, it was never mentioned again.

There had been a lot of talk lately about the Doctor and magic, but Littlenose was more concerned with the preparations for

the Sun Dance. This was the great mid-winter festival, like a huge party, with singing and dancing and feasting. Presents were given, and everyone had a marvellous time far into the night, even past bed-time for grownups. This year there was to be an extra treat. Occasionally the Doctor had been persuaded to give a demonstration of magic as part of the entertainment. His last appearance had been before Littlenose was old enough to attend the Sun Dance. In the few days left, the Doctor was very busy, and was quite huffy if anyone arrived at his cave with a sore stomach or toothache. All they got were some dried herbs or a quick drink of something discouraging from the Doctor's wife.

She was his assistant and nurse, and she spent most of her time out of sight at home. Littlenose thought that she was probably ashamed of being so ugly. She was tall and skinny, by Neanderthal standards, with a nose not much bigger than Littlenose's own. She might have been called Littlenose too, but her hair was long, straight and yellow, so she was called Goldie. It was rumoured that she came from a distant tribe and it was she who had taught the Doctor all he knew.

The Sun Dance came at last, and as usual it was even better than Littlenose remembered. When they had danced and sung themselves hoarse and even Littlenose had eaten himself to a standstill, the Old Man stepped forward and announced: "And now, for your delight and delectation, a fabulous feast of mystery and merriment proudly presented by the great . . . DOCTOR!" The Doctor swept into the circle with a flourish. He wore a cloak of some smooth, black fur, and a hood over his head. The hood covered his face so that his eyes shone out from a pair of holes. He looked mysterious and rather frightening. As the applause began to die away, the Old Man threw out an arm and shouted, "Assisted by the glamorous Goldie!"

The glamorous Goldie ran on to even louder applause and a great deal of whistling. In the torchlight she didn't really look all that ugly. Father stood up and cheered with the rest of the men. She wore two rabbit ears in her hair, while the rest consisted of all that was left of the rabbit . . . including the tail. "I hope she catches her death, dressed like that," sniffed Mother, giving Father one of her looks.

The magic show was everything Littlenose expected and more. Coloured pebbles appeared and reappeared. Old bones became bunches of flowers, and not one but *two* rabbits were pulled mysteriously from a fur hood. The audience cheered and clapped while Littlenose's eyes grew wider and wider at the wonder of it all. Then the Doctor and the glamorous Goldie carried forward what looked like the trunk of a tree. But as they set it up in front of the audience, Littlenose saw that the log had been hollowed out so that it was really only a

shell of very thin wood and bark. As it was laid on the ground he could also see that it had been split down the centre with the top half forming a sort of lid.

The Doctor held up his hand for silence. "I shall now attempt, with the assistance of the glamorous Goldie, one of the most hazardous feats of magic known. I must ask for complete silence. Thank you."

With a flourish he lifted the lid of the hollow log and held the glamorous Goldie by the hand while she climbed inside. She smiled prettily, waved, and lay down so that her head stuck out at one end and her feet at the other. The Doctor stooped down and picked up the biggest axe Littlenose had ever seen. The audience gasped as the Doctor swung it up without effort, and held their breath as he stood in the circle of torchlight which sparkled along the axe's sharp edge. Then, with a crash, the axe hurtled down on to the tree trunk and the glamorous Goldie!

Splinters flew in all directions as the blade buried itself in the ground. People screamed. Some fainted. Littlenose felt sick. But the Doctor was not finished yet. He quickly removed the axe and pulled the two halves of the log apart. There was a clear gap where the glamorous Goldie's middle should have been. Which wasn't surprising . . . and hardly magic!

What *was* surprising, and could only be magic was her nodding head and smiling face sticking out of one half, and her wriggling toes sticking out of the other. The audience was again silent as the Doctor quickly pushed the halves together. He waved his arms, shouted a magic word and raised the lid. The glamorous Goldie stood up and waved. There wasn't a mark on her. She bowed to the audience and Littlenose expected her top half to fall off. But it didn't, and the Doctor and the glamorous Goldie went off to thunderous applause.

In the weeks following the Sun Dance Littlenose could think of nothing else but magic. He even tried some, but without success. Things just refused to disappear, and Father almost split his sides laughing as Littlenose frantically waved an old bone in the air trying to turn it into a bunch of flowers. "Come on, Littlenose," he said, "you must do better than that. How about cutting a lady in half. I'm sure Mother would help. That is if you could get her inside a hollow log. Ha! Ha! Ha!" Mother said, "That's not funny."

"Just you wait," said Littlenose. "When I've learned to do a piece of magic you'll get the biggest surprise of your lives!"

After a few days Littlenose decided that his magic was getting nowhere. But he had an idea. He would find out how the Doctor did his. He couldn't very well ask him straight out, but if he could creep close enough to his cave he might see him at work. It was risky. He had once heard the story of a boy who had tried just this and had been turned into a frog!

Next morning Littlenose set off for the Doctor's cave. As he approached, he could hear voices from inside. He tip-toed to the entrance. The Doctor and his wife were seated with their backs to him, busy at some task . . . probably more magic. Littlenose edged closer, but whatever their task was, they were keeping it well hidden from intruders. He was about to leave when something caught his attention. Lying on a rocky ledge just inside the cave entrance was a stick, thick as a finger and about half the length of Littlenose's arm. It was stained with strange patterns, and Littlenose remembered that he had last seen it at the Sun Dance, when the Doctor had used it to wave or point at things he wanted to change into something else or to disappear. In a moment Littlenose had made up his mind. He would borrow the stick. He wouldn't ask for the loan of it. Just borrow it. In a flash the stick was under his hunting robe. Then Littlenose hurried home as fast as he could.

Slipping to the back of the cave he tried out the magic stick. He waved it, tapped it and shook it, but nothing disappeared. And nothing changed into anything else. But Littlenose wasn't downhearted. "Practice," he said to himself. "That's what I need." But before he could get any practice, he heard Father calling him.

"A herd of bison has been seen nearby," said Father, "and we're going out with a party to hunt them. Get your things. We're leaving immediately."

Littlenose put on his hunting robe and picked up his boy-size spear. He wondered about the magic stick for a moment, then decided to bind it along the shaft of the spear. This made it easy to carry and was unlikely to be noticed.

The hunters had barely left the caves before they realised that something odd was happening. The air was strangely mild, and there was a slight thaw, very unusual for this time of year. They trudged on through the woods, Littlenose and Two-Eyes bringing up the rear of the column. They stopped to rest for a moment, and Littlenose whispered to Two-Eyes, "Look, there's a robin," and pointed up into a tree. And at that second a great lump of melting snow slid from the tree and fell on one of the hunters with a thump. The man struggled to his feet and shook his fist at Littlenose. "That you up to your tricks?" he shouted. "Throwing things?"

"I didn't throw anything," said Littlenose. "I just pointed. Like that." He did it just as a pine branch, weakened by the weight of snow it was carrying, snapped with a loud crack and tumbled to the ground. The hunters all looked at Littlenose. They looked at the spear he was still pointing. *He* looked at the stick tied to the spear and began to wonder. However, after a bit of muttering among themselves the hunters went on their way, but kept a watchful eye on Littlenose. At length they reached a small valley with a frozen stream at the bottom. Nosey, the chief stalker, was warily inching his way across, but he didn't

feel at all safe. Littlenose stood with
Two-Eyes some way back from the stream
and watched. "I think you're too heavy to
cross there, Two-Eyes," he said, and
pointed with his spear. There was a loud
crack, then a wild yell from Nosey as the ice
broke under him and he vanished into the
freezing water. Littlenose dropped the spear
as if it were red hot.

While the hunters hauled a shivering
Nosey on to the bank, Littlenose untied the
stick and wondered what to do with it. He
had a feeling that just throwing it away
would be no good. He should never have
taken it without asking. He tucked it out of
sight in his furs, and planned to get it back
to its rightful owner just as soon as he
reached home. And it looked as if that
would be sooner than he'd expected. The
bison had gone, leaving no trace, and Nosey
was sneezing and shivering from his
ducking. The hunters decided to stop for the
night, and made a rough shelter out of tree
branches and hunting robes. The air had
turned heavy and clammy, while inky black
clouds began to pile up in the sky. They had
a cold supper, and while there was still
some light left Littlenose wandered off for a

stroll before turning in. He carried the magic stick under his robe, and had decided to try once more to make it work for him. After all, the disasters of earlier in the day could have just been chance. Perhaps.

When he was out of sight of the camp he picked up a handful of twigs and waved the stick over them. They were meant to turn into a bunch of flowers. Nothing happened, except that a large spot of rain fell on his nose. And that wasn't magic. He tried it on pebbles, but they remained obstinately unchanged. He even tapped himself on the head, and was relieved that he didn't turn into a frog. He gave up. The rain was beginning to fall heavily now, and the snow grew wet and mushy under his feet.

Littlenose shouted angrily at the stick, and shook it hard. "Call yourself magic? You're just an old bit of firewood. I dare you to do something magic!"

There was a blinding flash and a deafening bang. A solitary pine tree high on the hill in front of him was split from top to bottom by a jagged bolt of lightning. Littlenose fell to the ground in terror, and watched the smouldering remains of the tree, as the rain poured down about him and the thunder crashed and boomed about the sky.

Littlenose lay awake all night quaking with terror. Father and the other hunters were not sympathetic. "Fancy a big boy like you afraid of thunder," they laughed.

As soon as the hunting party reached home, Littlenose lost no time in returning the stick. He tried to sneak it back the way he had got it, but just as he was creeping up to the cave entrance a voice said: "What do you think you're playing at?" It was the Doctor. Littlenose was trapped. "This is it," he thought. "I'll be a frog any minute."

He stood up and held out the stick. "I was bringing this back. You see, it's like this. I was . . ."

But the Doctor cut him short. "Oh, thanks. Didn't know I'd dropped it. Didn't really matter." And he casually broke the stick into pieces and threw them in the fire.

Littlenose was aghast. The Doctor spoke again. "Here's something for your trouble." And he tossed a coloured pebble at Littlenose. He caught it . . . and it was an apple! "Now, off you go and don't bother me, Sonny. I've got a lot to do."

"Thank you," said Littlenose, thoroughly perplexed. He looked at the apple. Was it magic? He suddenly didn't care about magic any more, and he knew he managed to get into enough trouble without the aid of magic.

He started to run towards the cave, shouting, "Come on, Two-Eyes. I've got an apple. You can have half."

Bigfoot

One day, Father told Littlenose that they
were all going to spend a holiday with some
of their relatives. Littlenose didn't want to
go. And said so.

"You'll do as you're told for once," said
Father, "and like it."

"All right," said Littlenose, adding under
his breath, "but I won't like it."

The real trouble was that even Father
didn't think much of his sister's family
whom they would be visiting. Most
Neanderthal folk lived in tribes who made
their homes in caves. During the Ice Age,
life was very hard indeed, and
neighbours who could help each other in
times of trouble were essential. With water
being drawn from the river, firewood being
chopped, flints being chipped and all the
bustle and activity of a Neanderthal living
place going on from dawn to dusk, life was
hectic. Which was how people liked it. Most

of them, that is. For there were families who lived in remote places far from their nearest neighbours. That was how Littlenose's Uncle Juniper and his family lived. Littlenose had never met them but he knew that their home was far away in the mountains where the juniper bushes grew. Juniper berries were prized as medicine by the Neanderthal doctors, and every autumn the people of the mountains brought the season's fruit down to market. Littlenose's uncle was one of the best known, which accounted for his name. This much Littlenose had been told, but he had heard much more while lying awake at night listening to Mother and Father talking by the fire.

"How can anyone live like that? They do nothing. They see nothing. A crowd of yokels. Hill-billies. You can't even get decent conversation out of them. When I met Juniper at the market last week he hardly said a word from first to last."

"He probably couldn't get a word in edgeways," said Mother. "And he did say enough to invite us all to stay. In any case, if you don't like them why did you accept?"

"I wasn't thinking," groaned Father. "I

thought they only wanted Littlenose."

Next morning, after breakfast, Mother began the task of sorting out what they would need on holiday. Littlenose laid out his spear, his fire-making flints and his lucky coloured stone, and said, "I'm ready." But to his disgust Mother made him pack several pairs of clean furs as well. Looking at the final mound of baggage, Father said, "I think we might have been quicker just wrapping up the whole cave. We *are* only going to be away for three weeks, not the rest of our lives."

It was just getting light when they loaded Two-Eyes and set off next day. Uncle Juniper's home was one week's march due east of their own cave, and Father explained that if they walked with the rising sun in their faces and camped at evening with the setting sun at their backs they couldn't go wrong.

On the second day out, Father decided that they weren't travelling fast enough and had better break camp much earlier the following day. He roused everyone while it was still pitch dark, and set off. As they stumbled through the gloom, Mother said: "You're quite sure we're going the right way?"

"Am I in the habit of making mistakes?" said Father.

Mother just sniffed, while Littlenose nodded silently.

Then the sun rose . . . far to the left.

Father stopped and muttered something which nobody could make out, but which seemed to imply that the sun was in the wrong place. But they changed direction, and went on their way.

On the fourth day Father said: "We'll soon meet Uncle Juniper. When we stop tomorrow evening the sun should set exactly between two peaks. We have to wait at the pass between the peaks for Juniper to guide us the rest of the way."

Next evening as they made camp Littlenose watched the rim of the setting sun slip down between two sharp mountain tops. Before the light had completely gone

Father scratched a mark on the ground like a spear pointing towards the pass where tomorrow they hoped to find Uncle Juniper.

In fact Uncle Juniper found *them* next morning as they rested by a clear spring, and they arrived at the Juniper family cave before dusk.

It was very similar to the one in which Littlenose lived, with one marvellous difference. His cousins had a cave of their own, a smaller one that opened off the family cave. Here he was tucked up for the night with the three other boys, but none of them wanted to sleep. They whispered together in the dark exchanging boy-news. Littlenose told them of his home by the big river, of his visits to the market and his hunting lessons. He told them of bears and hyenas and sabre-toothed tigers. His cousins listened with amazement to the long stories of all his adventures. Then he asked, "What do *you* do around here?"

After a long pause, one cousin said: "Throw stones."

After another, even longer, pause the second cousin said: "Gather berries."

After a pause that was so long that Littlenose thought he had fallen asleep the third cousin said: "Throw more stones."

Littlenose's heart sank. This holiday was going to be every bit as dull as he imagined!

Next morning, after breakfast, Littlenose said, "What shall we do?" Without replying, his cousins stuck a row of sticks in the ground at the end of a stretch of green turf . . . and started to throw stones at them. They were very good at it, which Littlenose wasn't. They knocked the sticks flying every time, but Littlenose found that he could not even throw far enough, let alone straight and hard enough. Apart from the occasional squabble, they threw stones all that day. And the next. And the next. Littlenose was frantic with boredom, and his throwing arm ached. Then, he remembered the other thing his cousins did. "What about going berry picking?" he asked at lunch. His aunt looked up. "Yes," she said, "I could do with some blaeberries, but remember, don't go past the cairns." The cousins nodded.

Littlenose didn't know what a cairn was,
but he nodded too.

The berry picking was, if anything, more
boring than the stone throwing. There were
very few berries, and soon Littlenose's back
ached from stooping. He straightened up,
and saw a promising blaeberry patch some
way off. He was going towards it when he
heard a shout from the other boys: "Not
past the cairn!" He waved and walked on,
and they shouted again. Then he saw a
huge heap of large stones, as tall as he was.
Other heaps were in a long line across the
hillside. These must be the cairns. He
shrugged and turned back. "Why?" he
asked. His cousins looked at each other and
mumbled something that sounded like
"bigfoot".

"Who's Bigfoot?" asked Littlenose.

But his cousins wouldn't explain and just
hurried back to the cave.

After supper, Father took Littlenose on
one side and said, "I hope you haven't been
upsetting your cousins. The folk in these
parts are simple and superstitious. They say
if you go past the line of stone cairns the
local bogey man will grab you." Father
grinned. "He's tall, hairy, and you can
smell him a long way off. And he leaves
enormous footprints." Littlenose grinned
back at Father. It sounded very fanciful, but
still the line of cairns was intriguing. He
made up his mind to explore beyond them,
if only to show his simple cousins that there
was nothing to be afraid of.

Next morning, before anyone was awake,
Littlenose crept from the cave and made his
way to the blaeberry place. The early

morning mist made it difficult to see, and he
groped his way carefully forward. Suddenly
he stopped. A tall shape loomed in front of
him and his hair stood on end with fright.
But the figure didn't move. Then the mist
thinned in the breeze and he saw that it was
one of the stone cairns. Sighing with relief,
Littlenose pressed on. The mist rolled away
completely with the coming day, and he
found himself crossing a steep, bare
mountainside covered with stunted trees
and scrubby bushes. Patches of last winter's
snow lay here and there, and Littlenose was
scanning the ground ahead when he
noticed something odd about one of them.
There were huge footprints on it. But they
were old. The edges were blurred where the
sun had melted the snow, and the more he
looked at them the less sure he became that
they *were* footprints. All the talk of Bigfoot

43

was making his eyes play tricks on him. He went on his way.

Then he stopped at another snow patch. Here there were more marks like the last. But these were fresh, and most definitely footprints. Something very big had passed in front of him only a short time before! For the second time, Littlenose's hair stood on end. His mind went numb and he couldn't think. He jumped at a sudden sound. Something was coming out of the bushes. . . . In the split second before he took to his heels, Littlenose had a glimpse of something tall, shaggy and man-shaped looming out of the dark undergrowth. Littlenose flew downhill over snow, rock and gravel. Behind him the thing shambled swiftly in pursuit, plodding rapidly on enormous feet and short, powerful legs. And it was gaining on him.

The giant creature took one stride for every three of Littlenose's. He knew that he could never outrun it, but if he could hide, Father or Uncle Juniper would come looking for him. There was a dead tree straight ahead. It had been struck by lightning and stood white and bare against the dark green scrub. Littlenose ran the last

few steps, and dragged himself up to safety.

From his branch Littlenose looked down on the creature. It was twice as tall as a man, covered with shaggy fur, and had small eyes and a wide mouth with jagged teeth. And there was a terrible smell – like dead animals and damp caves all jumbled together. There was no mistake – this was Bigfoot!

When Bigfoot reached the tree he grabbed the trunk and shook it hard,

roaring with all his might. Littlenose shook
like a leaf in a gale, while Bigfoot tried to
climb after him. But the lower branches
weren't strong enough and broke under his
weight.

As he clung to the tree, Littlenose began
to think. It might be a long time before
anyone came to his rescue, and it seemed
unlikely that the dead tree would stand
much of Bigfoot's shaking. He had to do
something before the whole lot crashed to
the ground. He rummaged furiously in his
furs and fished out his fire-making flints.
Animals were afraid of fire and Bigfoot was
at least part animal. Quickly he struck a
spark on to the dead leaves clinging to a
withered branch. The leaves caught fire and
the branch became a torch. Breaking it off,
Littlenose leaned forward and carefully
dropped the flaming branch. But Bigfoot
sidestepped, and as the burning torch fell to
the ground picked it up and threw it into
the bushes. "He's not all *that* animal,"
thought Littlenose in dismay. There seemed
no point in lighting another branch, and he
looked around in despair for a new idea.
Then he realised that Bigfoot's attention
had wandered. He was sniffing loudly, and

swinging his head from side to side.
Littlenose saw that a grey pall of smoke was
blowing across the hillside. The torch had
set fire to the undergrowth. The smoke
became thicker, and swirled around the
foot of the tree until Bigfoot was only a dim,
coughing shape. This was Littlenose's
chance. He slithered to the ground, and
under cover of the smoke ran as hard as he
could. Behind him he heard thudding
footsteps as Bigfoot took up the chase again.
But now Littlenose could see the line of
cairns. He passed the first cairn and glanced
over his shoulder. Bigfoot was almost on
him. Then he heard a voice: "Get down,
Littlenose!" And at the same time
something whizzed past his ear. Littlenose
threw himself flat and heard Bigfoot roaring
angrily behind him. Raising his head he
saw a shower of well-aimed stones flying
through the air while Bigfoot tried to fend
them off with wildly waving arms. At last
the monstrous creature gave up and
stumbled back up the mountainside and out
of sight, leaving behind a trail of huge
footprints and a dreadful smell. The cousins
threw their remaining stones for luck before
escorting Littlenose back to the cave.

The grownups weren't told of his adventure.

As he was leaving with Father, Mother and Two-Eyes at the end of the holiday Uncle Juniper said to Littlenose, "Well, and how would you like to live here with us in peace and quiet?"

"Actually," replied Littlenose, "I think the excitement would be too much for me. Goodbye, and thank you for having me."

Littlenose's Rhinoceros

Littlenose's people hunted animals for food.
And some of the animals hunted
Neanderthal folk. Bears, lions and wolves
were quite common during the Ice Age, and
people soon learned their ways and how to
avoid them. There was also the sabre-
toothed tiger! The sabre-toothed tiger was
very strong, very fierce, and luckily very
rare.

Father came home one day from a short
hunting trip with some venison . . . and very
disturbing news. As they had neared home,
the hunters had crossed a trail of enormous
paw prints, and realised they were the
tracks of a sabre-toothed tiger. Father spoke
very firmly to Littlenose: "Now pay
attention to what I say. Stay close to home
and don't wander. The tiger may only be
passing through; on the other hand it may
have found a den nearby. Remember!"

And Littlenose promptly forgot.

Luckily the other members of the tribe were more careful, and took care that no one, including Littlenose, went too far from home. But the days became weeks, and soon a whole summer had passed without another sign of the tiger. The tribe had even stopped talking about it, and when Littlenose wandered off into the woods with his boy-size hunting spear no one tried to stop him. Because of the tiger there had been very little hunting recently and Littlenose was thoroughly tired of rabbit, pigeon and other small game. Like everyone else in the tribe he fancied something tastier. He thought a nice fat deer would do.

But he couldn't even find a nice fat mouse! The biggest thing he saw was a black beetle, and even that scurried away before he could catch it. Studying the ground for broken twigs, footprints and any other signs of game, Littlenose worked his way deep into the woods . . . and out of the other side. Beyond the trees stretched a flat plain, then there was a patch of thick bushes, which were as empty as the woods had been. And after the bushes the land stretched bare and empty to the horizon. Littlenose walked on a little farther then

realised that he was hungry. It must be
nearly suppertime. He would be in trouble
if he were late, so he started walking in the
direction of home. But this wasn't fast
enough, and he started to run. He ran until
he reached the bushes. And now he forgot
one of the most important Neanderthal
rules. He didn't look first! He pushed
through, burst out on the other side . . . and
found himself face to face with a woolly
rhinoceros. Both stopped in their tracks –
Littlenose was too frightened, and the
rhinoceros was too short-sighted!

Then it realised there was a boy barring
its path, and put down its head to charge.
Pawing the ground, it pointed its long horns
straight at Littlenose and blinked its angry
little red eyes through its fur. It had taken
half a step forward when it stopped. Then it
took a step back. And another. As the gap
between them widened, Littlenose, still
afraid, took a cautious step forward. Again
the woolly rhinoceros moved back. "It's
afraid of me," said Littlenose to himself, and
waved his spear above his head. At this the
enormous animal almost fell over itself as it
whirled round and fled headlong. Without a
moment's hesitation Littlenose followed.

Back into the long grass galloped the
rhinoceros. After it raced Littlenose, his
spear gripped firmly and all trace of fright
gone. "I must look fiercer than I thought,"
he gasped. "If I can catch it, the whole
tribe will have meat for a month."
Brandishing his boy-size spear he let out a
wild yell.

It was easy to follow the woolly
rhinoceros as it trampled a broad track
through the long grass. Straight through the
woods it went without slowing down,
crushing small trees and saplings as it
passed. Far behind, running and stumbling
along the trampled track came Littlenose,
still waving his spear and crying: "Stop!
Come back! You can't get away! I'll get
you!"

Meanwhile, back at the caves it was almost supper time, and there was the usual bustle. Women fetched water from the river and men carried wood for the fires. Some of the families had started eating when the most extraordinary noise was heard. Everyone paused to listen. They heard a loud galloping sound and a smashing and crashing of twigs and branches. Above all that they could make out a voice shouting: "Stop my rhinoceros! Stop it! Quick, help me catch it! It's mine! Stop it!"

By this time all the tribe were on their feet. Then someone shouted: "RUN FOR YOUR LIVES!" as something huge and woolly, hung all over with twigs and leaves, surged over the brow of the hill and thundered towards them. Right into the middle of the tribe the rhinoceros charged! No one was hurt, but fires were scattered, pots broken and suppers strewn all over the ground. A bear skin pegged out to dry tangled around a woolly leg, while a washing line of furs caught on a horn and was borne away streaming behind the rhinoceros as it disappeared in a cloud of dust. Then a smaller (and if anything noisier) creature rushed from the woods. It was Littlenose.

"That was MY rhinoceros," he panted. "You were meant to catch him. I've chased him and chased him, and if you lot had caught hold of him there was enough meat and more for everyone!" And he jumped up and down with rage. The tribe jumped up and down with rage too. They had one idea – to get their hands on Littlenose. They crowded round him and he looked up at a ring of very angry faces.

And next moment he was alone!

Where there had been a whole tribe standing in the wreckage of spilt suppers and scattered fires now there was no one. Littlenose saw that the people had vanished into their caves and were busy rolling boulders across the entrances. Was the rhinoceros coming back? Before he could find out he felt himself grabbed by the arm and run towards his own cave while Father's voice bellowed angrily in his ear: "Stupid boy, do you want to be eaten?" And he pointed to the woods. There, stalking majestically was a sleek, tawny creature. It swished a long tail as it came, and opened an enormous pair of jaws filled with sharp fangs. It was a sabre-toothed tiger.

Littlenose sat down hard on the floor of the cave while Father piled rocks across the opening. When the last chink had been blocked, Father turned to Littlenose. "Did you think," he shouted, "it was YOU that a big thing like that was running from? It more likely saw the tiger behind your back. Catch a woolly rhinoceros! Indeed!"

"What do we do now?" asked Littlenose in a small voice.

"Wait," said Father. "If the tiger isn't too hungry it may go away. If it *is* . . ." He didn't even bother to finish the sentence.

All this time the sabre-toothed tiger had been making its way towards the barricaded caves. There was not a sound. But there were some interesting scents. Like a

customer in a café studying the menu it paced slowly from cave to cave. It paused at each one and had a good long sniff, while inside the owners cowered and held their breath. It seemed like a lifetime, then Father, Mother, Two-Eyes and Littlenose heard padding footsteps and heavy breathing coming through the cracks in the barrier; and they squeezed as far to the back of the cave as they could and waited.

Outside the cave the tiger took a long, deep sniff. It caught the scent of man. And woman. It could also smell mammoth. Inside, Two-Eyes could smell tiger, and shook so much that his ears flapped. The sabre-toothed tiger enjoyed a piece of mammoth from time to time, but now its heart was set on something much more tasty. Slowly it made out the scent it had been seeking. Boy! Fresh Neanderthal boy! Like the one it had been stalking when that stupid rhinoceros had blundered along and spoilt everything! The tiger had one last, satisfying sniff to make absolutely sure, purred loudly in anticipation, then hurled itself at the rock barricade.

The whole cave shook, while those inside shook even more as the roars of the hungry

tiger made their heads ring. Mother had *her*
head under a pile of furs and Father
carefully kept Two-Eyes between himself
and the cave entrance. Again and again the
sabre-toothed tiger attacked the rocks, and
each time they heaved and shuddered. For
a long time the barricade held firm, but
then gaps began to appear as smaller stones
came loose and tumbled out. Soon, patches
of evening sky were visible. Then a
particularly large stone fell to the floor of
the cave and a pair of fierce yellow eyes
glared in. The eyes disappeared and were
replaced by a huge paw. Carefully the paw
groped through the opening and felt about
inside. Long, cruel claws slashed about in
the air, and some more stones fell to the
ground. But still the tiger couldn't reach far
enough inside to catch anyone, and it
pulled out its paw and planned its next
move.

Now, Littlenose had been doing some
planning on his own. He could just
remember the day that he and his family
had first come to live in this cave. It had
really belonged to a family of ferocious
bears, but while the bears were out hunting,
Father had barricaded the entrance just as

it was now. Then they had fought the bears
off with sticks and stones, and finally with
fire until the bears ran away and were
never seen again. There was an ominous
growling as Littlenose scrabbled around on
the floor of the cave looking for something
to make fire. He could find only a handful
of twigs and small branches, but he began
desperately to strike.sparks with his flints.

The sabre-toothed tiger gave a terrible
roar, hurled its weight against the barrier,
and reached in and clutched about with
sharp claws. But by this time the torch was
alight. Littlenose let out a wild yell, rushed
forward, and jabbed the torch at the tiger's
paw. There was a scream and a smell of
singed fur as the paw disappeared.

"It's gone," Littlenose shouted to Father. "Wild animals are afraid of fire."

But this was one wild animal that didn't know it was meant to be afraid, and came roaring back. Again it reached inside, and again Littlenose struck out with his burning twigs. The cave was now full of smoke and dust so that when it drew back yet again Littlenose clambered on to the barricade and peered out of the hole to see if it had at last gone. It was dusk, so he held the torch at arm's length, straining his eyes. Next moment he thought his arm had been pulled off. From nowhere, it seemed, the tiger leapt up and slashed at the flames, knocking the torch from Littlenose's hand and Littlenose himself into a heap on the floor of the cave. Half dazed, he limped over to his own special corner, for he hadn't given up yet. Rummaging under his sleeping furs he pulled out his hunting spear. "Don't give up hope. I'll save us all," he cried.

As the tiger leapt at the hole in the rocks this time it was met not by a smoky torch but by a sharp flint spear point. Littlenose jabbed furiously and heard the tiger howl with rage. It drew back and charged, and

again had its ribs pricked for its pains.
Furiously, it reached inside again, trying to
catch what was doing the pricking, and had
its paw jabbed. Inside, Littlenose jabbed
away like mad. Sometimes he missed the
tiger, but more often he scored a hit.
However, instead of driving the tiger away,
he was making it more and more angry. Its
evening meal was just on the other side of
this pile of stones, and it was not giving up
now. It stood up on its hind legs and began
to push the smaller rocks at the top of the
barricade. As it did this Littlenose
scrambled up on his side to try and strike
downwards with his spear through some of
the bigger gaps. The whole rock pile was
becoming very shaky. Then Littlenose felt
the stones move under his feet. He tried to

jump clear, but he was too late. With a loud rumble the rock barrier collapsed outwards, and Littlenose found himself sprawling on top of an untidy heap of stones.

He looked around. Father came cautiously from the cave and lit a fresh torch. There was no sign of the sabre-toothed tiger. Mother and Two-Eyes crept out looking carefully around them, and soon the rest of the tribe took down their own barricades and crept out likewise.

"It's gone," they said.

Littlenose leapt up on to the heap of stones. "Yes, it's gone," he shouted. "And I did it. I chased it away. All by myself."

Father said: "Stop that row, and help clear up the mess." That was typical of Father. Always spoiling things for people. Littlenose was lifting a particularly large stone when something struck him as odd. In the torchlight he bent down and felt with his hand. There was something soft. He lifted a few more stones, and looked again. It was *fur*. Long, tawny fur! He called to Father, and between them they cleared the remaining rocks. And there lay the sabre-toothed tiger, sprawled on the ground. Cold, stone dead.

Again Littlenose danced up and down, this time shouting, "I killed it. I pushed the rocks on top of the sabre-toothed tiger."

"If it hadn't been for you," everyone cried, "it wouldn't have come here in the first place, nor the woolly rhinoceros, if it comes to that."

But, that night while Littlenose was asleep, Father took his sharp flint knife and skinned the tiger. And from that day on Littlenose's was the only cave with a tiger-skin rug in front of the fire.

Littlenose to the Rescue

Littlenose's people, the Neanderthal folk, were really not very clever, and like a lot of people were suspicious of those who were. As far as they were concerned the Neanderthal way of doing things was the only right and proper way. Even people who *looked* different were thought slightly dangerous. And one person who was all of these things was Littlenose's Uncle Redhead. He could do things that most Neanderthal men never even heard of, and he also had flaming red hair. Neanderthal folk were generally very dark. Nobody actually threatened Uncle Redhead or said anything impolite to his face, but there was a lot of talk among the tribe when he wasn't there. This made Littlenose very angry, and he would shout, "You shouldn't say things like that about my Uncle Redhead. He's the cleverest person in the whole world."

"There's such a thing as being too

clever," he was told. The only other person who seemed to like Uncle Redhead was Mother. And he was her brother.

One day Uncle Redhead dropped in for a visit. "Just passing through," he said.

"Good," said Father.

After supper, Littlenose went for a stroll before bedtime with Uncle Redhead. They walked along the river bank chatting about this and that, then sat on a rock by the water's edge and watched the ripples. Uncle Redhead turned to Littlenose. "Tell me what you've been doing since I last saw you," he said. Littlenose mentioned a few things, then went on to describe his holiday with Uncle Juniper and his family in the mountains.

"I thought it would be dull," he said, "and it was to begin with. Then I had a narrow escape. I don't ever want to go back there again."

He described the evil creature which had left the huge footprints in the snow and had chased him over the mountainside. "Uncle Juniper's boys called it a bigfoot." He had told no one else until now, and he half expected Uncle Redhead to laugh. But his uncle nodded his head and said: "I've come

across those creatures myself. They don't
half smell." Littlenose nodded agreement.
"The northern tribes have another name for
them," went on Uncle Redhead.
"Something like 'disgusting snowmen'.
Very odd. Anyway, how did you escape?"

"The boys threw stones," said Littlenose.
"I've never seen anyone throw stones as far
or as hard as they did. I wish that I could."

"As far as this?" said Uncle Redhead,
tossing a pebble into the river.

"Much farther," said Littlenose.

"How about this, then," said Uncle
Redhead. "Watch that log." And he
pointed to a large piece of driftwood just
visible on the far side of the river. Then he
stepped behind Littlenose. Littlenose kept
his eyes glued to the log. There was a sound
behind him and a stone whirred over his
head. Straining his eyes, Littlenose just
made out the spurt in the water beside the
log where the stone had landed.

Littlenose said nothing. He just stared
open-mouthed and open-eyed in
amazement. Nobody, not even Uncle
Redhead, could throw a stone as far as that!
He turned to Uncle Redhead, who grinned.
"Watch again, Littlenose," he said. "Watch

that tall tree, where the herons nest."
Littlenose again peered across the river to
where the white shapes of the herons could
just be seen standing guard over their
ragged nests in the topmost branches. Again
there was a noise from Uncle Redhead and
again a stone whizzed over Littlenose's
head. But this time it was followed by the
angry squawk of enraged herons as the
stone zipped through the tree branches.

Uncle Redhead laughed and said,
"Wouldn't you like to be able to throw
stones like that?"

"Yes, PLEASE!" said Littlenose.

"Well, come here and I'll teach you," said his uncle, at the same time holding up a curious object. It was a leather pouch, with two long rawhide thongs dangling from it. Uncle Redhead took a pebble, placed it in the pouch, and whirled it round and round his head. Suddenly he let go of one of the thongs and next moment the pebble was flying across the river so fast and far it was almost out of sight.

"It's called a sling," said Uncle Redhead. "Some of the Straightnose tribes use them for hunting. *Our* people won't touch them. Too new-fangled for them, I suppose. But now it's your turn."

Littlenose held the sling carefully in his right hand as Uncle Redhead showed him, and placed a stone in the pouch. Then he swung it round his head. Faster and faster he whirled it until Uncle Redhead yelled, "Now! Let go!" And Littlenose *let* go. Completely. So that the sling as well as the stone landed in the water. Luckily Littlenose had not swung it very hard, and it was close enough to the bank for Uncle Redhead to hook it out with a long stick.

Next time Littlenose was thinking so hard about not letting go completely that he forgot to let go at all. The thongs wound round and round his head and the stone gave him a nasty bang on the ear.

With his next attempt he just missed Uncle Redhead's eye, but it was a beginning. By the time they returned to the cave Littlenose could send a stone much farther and harder than before, and more or less in the direction he intended. Before he left, Uncle Redhead said seriously: "A sling is not a toy. It is a dangerous weapon. You must only practise where there is no chance of anyone being in the way. As a hunter you should find it very useful."

As a junior hunter, Littlenose was supposed to put in a lot of practice in things like spear throwing and fire lighting and tracking. Father usually had to remind him, but now, to his amazement, Littlenose spent all day and every day out of doors practising. What Father didn't know was that it was sling practice. Littlenose didn't dare tell him. He had a feeling that Father wouldn't approve. As the weeks went by, Littlenose became more and more expert, until he could hit an oak tree at a hundred paces. He felt very pleased with himself as he made his way home one evening. "You

know, Two-Eyes," he said to his pet mammoth, "I definitely think that I'm ready to take my sling hunting. Tomorrow!"

Next morning, after breakfast, Littlenose strolled out of the cave. He wasn't carrying his spear, and Mother asked, "Where are you going, dear? Aren't you practising?"

"Not today," he replied. "I'm just going for a walk with Two-Eyes."

"Well, be good and don't be late," said Mother. She didn't see the sling, tucked carefully out of sight inside Littlenose's furs.

They followed the trail by the river, then turned away to climb through the woods towards the high country where the best hunting was to be found. But they saw nothing. Littlenose thought this very strange, and even Two-Eyes began to look around, and sniff the air. He was acting very uneasily, and stopped more and more frequently to sniff the breeze and to spread his big ears to catch suspicious sounds. "Come on, Two-Eyes," said Littlenose. "There's nothing." But Two-Eyes' steps began to drag, and he went slower and slower until he stopped. He trumpeted softly and nudged Littlenose with his furry

trunk. "It's too soon to go home," said
Littlenose. "Tell you what. We'll have a
rest among those trees over there."

The trees formed a small wood, and
Littlenose found a comfortable grassy bank
where he lay down, but Two-Eyes refused
to rest. He paced up and down, sniffing and
listening, and growing more agitated every
moment.

At last Littlenose could stand it no
longer. He jumped up. "For goodness' sake,
Two-Eyes. . . ." Then, faintly, as if coming
from a long way off, he could hear strange
noises. It was a confused mixture of animal
sounds and men's voices, with bangings and
rattlings and the pounding of hooves.

Quickly, Littlenose climbed to the top of the tallest tree in the wood and peered across country. It was a moment before he saw anything, then he made out a long cloud of dust stretching across the horizon. "A stampede," thought Littlenose. "Probably bison. Well, this is the safest place to be." He called down to Two-Eyes, "Stay where you are. You'll be all right." But Two-Eyes was gone. Littlenose had a glimpse of him running as fast as his short hairy legs could carry him away from the approaching dust cloud.

The first warning that all was not well was the appearance of the stampeding animals. They were elk! At least two were. But there were half a dozen horses, and a woolly rhinoceros. Then some bison. Then several deer. More and more appeared, charging madly along, and all mixed up together. The noise of hooves was deafening as the huge crowd of galloping creatures thundered round and through the wood. They neighed, roared, whinnied, squealed and bellowed, and Littlenose wondered what made them run. Bison, he knew, stampeded often, and other animals might flee from something like a grass fire. But there was no sign of smoke. As the last small deer rushed under the tree and out again into the open, Littlenose saw the reason. A long line of men was advancing. They were rattling sticks and spears together, or beating on clay pots with skins stretched across the tops to make a loud booming. The men shouted and whooped as they drove the frightened animals before them. It was a hunting party.

A *Straightnose* hunting party!

Sometimes the Neanderthal folk used stampeding as a way of hunting, but not very successfully. More often than not the animals got the wrong idea, and it was the hunters who had to stampede to safety! But the Straightnoses were clever and highly organised. From high in the tree Littlenose watched the line of men pass swiftly beneath him and on across the plain in the wake of their quarry. What they would do next, and how they would catch the animals he didn't know. But somewhere out there was Two-Eyes, and he was as sure as the elk and the bison to be caught by the Straightnoses. Littlenose scrambled down and ran after the hunters as hard as he could.

By the time that Littlenose emerged into

the open the line of Straightnose hunters
had passed out of sight and the sound of the
animals had died away. The trail was easy
to follow, and Littlenose panted along over
the trampled grass and deep hoof prints.
After a time he became aware that the
noises in front were getting louder. They
seemed to come from a fold in the ground
which formed a broad hollow. Littlenose
crept towards the hollow and very
cautiously peered over the rim. He saw an
incredible sight. The hollow was packed
with animals. Elk, horses, rhinoceros and
deer milled about, bellowing and squealing.
The Straightnoses had set up tall wooden
stakes in the ground round the edge of the

hollow, and had tied long branches between to make a rough fence. One end was open, and the Straightnoses were driving in the last animals with loud yells and much waving of spears. As the last deer fled in panic into the trap, half a dozen brawny hunters lifted a long loose section of fence into place and fixed it fast with ropes. Then the Straightnoses turned to where a fire was burning some distance away and where they evidently intended to camp for the night.

Littlenose watched the trapped animals. They made plenty of noise, but didn't seem to be trying to escape. The fence looked quite flimsy, but even great beasts like the rhinoceros and elk were too frightened to realise it. But Littlenose was more interested in looking for one particular animal. It seemed unlikely that Two-Eyes had escaped, so he must be somewhere in there. In the dust it was hard to pick out something as small as a young mammoth, and Littlenose was daring to hope that Two-Eyes might have just got away when above the din he heard a familiar squeaky trumpeting. Directly below him he saw a small black shape pressed against the bars of the trap, and a short trunk waving forlornly through a gap. Somehow he must rescue Two-Eyes. But how? The Straightnoses would spot him the moment that he appeared in the hollow, and in any case he knew that he was too small to open the gate or make a gap for Two-Eyes to squeeze through. He didn't even have his spear. But he did have his sling. Tucked inside his furs so that he had forgotten all about it.

Quickly Littlenose picked up a stone, fitted it into the sling and sent it whizzing down into the hollow. It struck a rhinoceros on the ear. The rhino squealed, then jumped and butted a large elk with its horns. The elk lashed out with its hooves, missed the rhino, but caught a horse in the ribs. The horse went mad, snapping and biting at everything, and in a moment there was uproar. The hunters came running and saw the animals in the trap fighting and struggling among themselves. They also saw that the fence was beginning to give way as the heavy creatures crashed into it. Then one hunter shouted and pointed. A whole section of stakes and branches was sagging to the ground. The Straightnoses began to run as again the animals stampeded . . . with the Straightnoses in front this time!

Littlenose screamed: "Up here, Two-Eyes!"
And the little mammoth heard his voice
above the din and scrambled out of the
hollow to join him.

Soon all the animals were gone. So were
the Straightnoses and their camp. The trap
was just a scattered mess of broken sticks.

Littlenose put his sling carefully back
inside his furs. Then he took Two-Eyes'
trunk in his hand, and together they set off
for home, supper and bed.

Other books in the same series:
Arabel's Raven
The Barrow Lane Gang
The Bread Bin
Brer Rabbit Stories
Dragons
The Elm Street Lot
The Escaped Black Mamba
Icelandic Stories
The Impecunious Hero
Jack Stories
The Lion and other Animal Stories
Littlenose
Littlenose the Fisherman
Littlenose Moves House
Littlenose the Hero
Littlenose the Hunter
Lizzie Dripping
Lizzie Dripping and the Little Angel
Lizzie Dripping by the Sea
The Moon on the Water
The Quest for Olwen
Robin Hood
The Saturday Man
Stories from Ireland
Stories from Norway
Stories from Poland
Stories from Russia
Stories from Scotland
Stories from Wales
Voyage of the Griffin
The Wilkses
Wizards are a Nuisance

Jackanory Hardbacks
The Adventures of Brer Rabbit
The Adventures of Littlenose
Lizzie Dripping
Lizzie Dripping Again
The Pedlar of Swaffham
Tom Tit Tot